MW00885828

Linda

Bayside

CODY

The Teeny, Tiny Alpaca

Amber & Cody

By

Amber Isaac

Copyright © 2015 Amber Isaac.

All rights reserved. No part of this book may be used or reproduced by any means, graphic, electronic, or mechanical, including photocopying, recording, taping or by any information storage retrieval system without the written permission of the publisher except in the case of brief quotations embodied in critical articles and reviews.

Archway Publishing books may be ordered through booksellers or by contacting:

Archway Publishing
1663 Liberty Drive
Bloomington, IN 47403
www.archwaypublishing.com
1 (888) 242-5904

Because of the dynamic nature of the Internet, any web addresses or links contained in this book may have changed since publication and may no longer be valid. The views expressed in this work are solely those of the author and do not necessarily reflect the views of the publisher, and the publisher hereby disclaims any responsibility for them.

ISBN: 978-1-4808-1636-7 (sc)
ISBN: 978-1-4808-1638-1 (hc)
ISBN: 978-1-4808-1637-4 (e)

Print information available on the last page.

Archway Publishing rev. date: 07/07/2015

visit Cody's website:
www.codyalpaca.com

Meet Cody.
Cody is a baby ALPACA.

Cody has long legs and a long neck. When she talks, she says "Hmmmmm?"

When Cody was born, she was very, very tiny.

Cody felt happy
and loved.
She was proud
of who she was.

Everyday, Cody
worked hard to grow
big and strong.

Soon, Cody was old enough to play with other baby alpacas.

When she went outside, she saw that the other babies were much bigger than she was.

The kids had never seen such a teeny, tiny alpaca! "Why are you so little?" they asked. "Didn't you grow?"

Cody's feelings were hurt. She had worked very hard to grow, but she still wasn't as big as everyone else.

Cody was very upset.
She ran home to hide.

The next day, Cody didn't want to go outside again. She was afraid they would laugh at her for being so little.

She told her mama that she had a tummy ache & needed to stay home.

Cody's mama knew she
didn't have a tummy ache.
"Why is my girl so sad?"
she asked little Cody.

"They said I was
teeny, tiny."
Cody cried.

"But Cody, it's ok to be tiny" her mama said. "It's part of what makes you unique. Unique means you're one of a kind."

"Give the other children a chance to get to know you better."

Cody thought about it. She had really been looking forward to playing with the other babies.

But they were so much bigger, especially one boy named Cori, who towered above all the others.

"...and Ghostlight has a white face..."

"...and Bialystock has a hard name..."

"...and Mayzie has fuzzy ears..."

"...and Fastrada has a brown spot..."

"In fact, each of the other babies has something unique about them, just like I do!!"

Suddenly, Cody couldn't wait to go play. Maybe her tummy didn't hurt so much after all.

Cody took a deep breath
and ran back to the pasture.

The other babies saw her and started asking her questions.

"I was born very little," Cody answered,
"but I've grown a lot since then."

"Wow! That's really cool!" the other alpacas squealed. "We've never met an alpaca as teeny, tiny as you. You're fun!"

Cody had a wonderful day playing
in the pasture with her new friends.

At the end of the day, she
happily skipped home!

She decided she always wanted to be unique & special.

What made
her different,
now made her

HAPPY!!

So, now Cody wants to ask you:
"What makes you unique?"

The End